STERLING CHILDREN'S BOOKS
New York

An Imprint of Sterling Publishing Co., Inc.
1166 Avenue of the Americas
New York, NY 10036

ISBN 978-1-4549-2573-6

Distributed in Canada by Sterling Publishing Co., Inc.
C/o Canadian Manda Group, 664 Annette Street
Toronto, Ontario, Canada M6S 2C8
Distributed in the United Kingdom by GMC Distribution Services
Castle Place, 166 High Street, Lewes, East Sussex, England BN7 1XU
Distributed in Australia by NewSouth Books
45 Beach Street, Coogee, NSW 2034, Australia

For information about custom editions, special sales, and premium and corporate purchases,
please contact Sterling Special Sales at 800-805-5489 or specialsales@sterlingpublishing.com.

Manufactured in China

Lot #:
2 4 6 8 10 9 7 5 3 1
07/17

www.sterlingpublishing.com

Designed by Heather Kelly
The artwork for this book was created digitally.

**FOR FRANCES, WHO I KNOW WOULD SHARE WITH A BEAR.
ALL MY LOVE, GRANDMA.**

WILLA
AND THE BEAR

BY PHILOMENA O'NEILL

STERLING CHILDREN'S BOOKS
New York

Willa loves her rag doll, Rosie. Rosie is extra special—handmade for Willa by Grandma Bibbie.

Willa and Rosie have picnics in the springtime . . .

. . . and pick berries all summer long.

Come fall, they gather leaves into piles
big enough for them to leap into.

When winter comes and the ground glistens with snow, Willa tucks Rosie in cozily for the ride to Grandma's birthday dinner.

Crissh, crissh. The sled slices through the snow. The horse tosses
his head and huffs, jingling the reins. Momma, Papa, and Willa
sit tight as the sled rocks from side to side.

They enter the woods just as the sun starts to set.
Papa lights a lamp, and shadows dance between the trees.

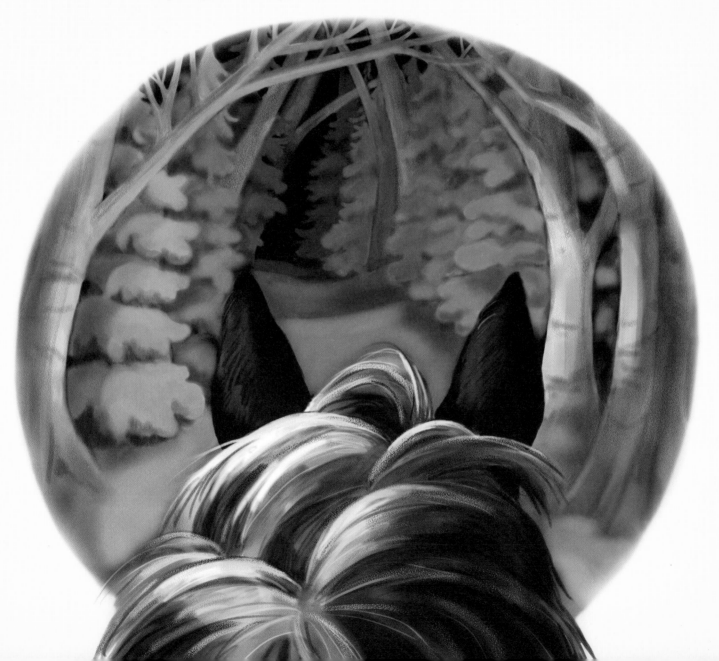

"I wish we were there," Willa sighs.

"Let's sing so the journey goes faster," suggests Momma.

The sled bounces high over a bump in the road. Willa laughs with delight and snuggles back into her blankets.

When Willa reaches down for her doll, she cries out, "Rosie's not here!"

She could be anywhere—hidden in the shadows of trees or in a patch of tall grass. Momma and Papa and Willa search and search . . .

. . . but Rosie is nowhere to be found. Frost
crackles under their boots, and a bitter wind snaps
at their faces. "It's getting late," says Momma
softly, turning Willa back toward the sled.

Snork, snork. Snuffle, snuffle. Sniff, sniff.

Missing Rosie hurts much, much more than the sting of cold air against Willa's face.

Willa is still thinking of Rosie when the sled stops at last.

"There, there," says Grandma Bibbie. "I have a new present for you."

Willa smiles to see the bear that matches Grandpa's new trousers.

But Willa can't help wondering about
Rosie all alone in the cold, dark woods.
Is she lonely? Is she afraid?

"Papa! A bear!"

Papa peers outside. He doesn't see a bear, but he does see *something* . . .

Willa can't believe it! It's Rosie!

"That bear must be a friend of yours,"
says Grandma Bibbie with a smile.

Willa hugs her two friends close.

"'Bye, Grandma Bibbie! 'Bye, Grandpa!"

Crissh, crissh.

The sled slices the snow once more as Momma, Papa, and Willa make their way back home.

Shadows move with the swinging of the lamp.

"Over there, Rosie," says Willa quietly. "Do you see that?"

Willa thinks she recognizes the shaggy round shadow.

Willa kisses the small bear that matches Grandpa's trousers.

"My friend will love you," she whispers.

And he does.